Alesia

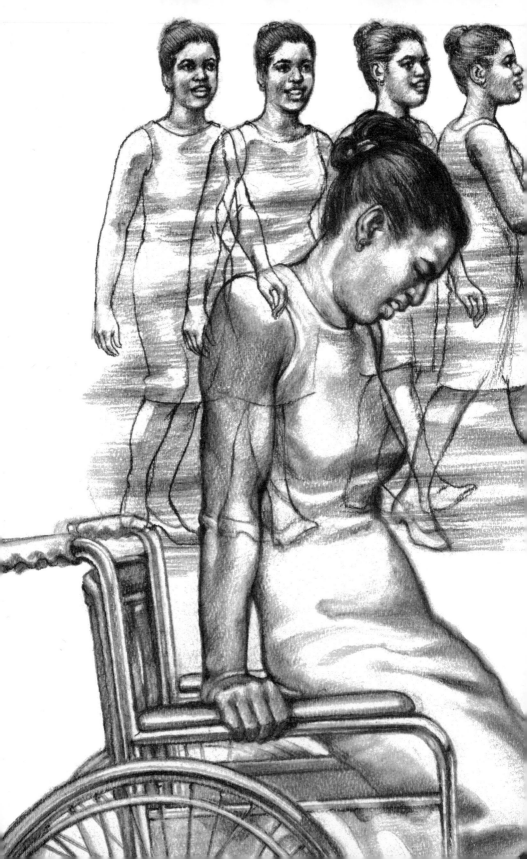

By Eloise Greenfield
and Alesia Revis

ALESIA

Drawings by George Ford

Photographs by
Sandra Turner Bond

Philomel Books

Text copyright © 1981
by Eloise Greenfield and Alesia Revis
Drawings copyright © 1981 by George Ford
Photographs copyright © 1981 by Sandra Turner Bond

All rights reserved.
Published by Philomel Books,
a division of The Putnam Publishing Group,
200 Madison Avenue,
New York, N.Y. 10016.
Printed in the United States of America.

Library of Congress Cataloging in Publication Data

Greenfield, Eloise.

Alesia.

Summary: A physically handicapped girl discusses
her daily activities, the accident which left her
crippled, and her feelings about her disability.

1. Revis, Alesia—Juvenile literature. 2. Physically
handicapped children—United States—
Biography—Juvenile literature. [1. Physically
handicapped] I. Revis, Alesia. II. Ford, George
Cephas.
III. Bond, Sandra Turner. IV. Title.
RD796.R48G73   362.4'3'0924 [B]   81-5862
ISBN 0-399-20831-3   AACR2

*To Mama and Daddy, Alexis and Allen,
Grandma and Granddaddy,
because they have done so much for me*

and

*To all of my other family and friends
who have helped me.*

A. R.

Alesia

The Accident

It happened in Washington, D. C., on the evening of August 29, 1972. Nine-year-old Alesia was having a good time. She and her friend Percy were racing on their bikes, flying down the alley to see which one could go faster. When they reached the street, Percy took a quick look for cars and kept going. Alesia was right behind him.

It wasn't a street that was heavily traveled, only a few cars came through now and then. But a car *was* coming that day, at just that very moment, headed straight toward Alesia. She never saw it. When they got her to Providence Hospital, she was pronounced DOA—dead on arrival.

But Alesia didn't die. She's seventeen now and very much alive. This book is her story.

Eloise Greenfield
August 1980

Wed., March 19, 1980

This morning I woke up and looked at the clock. It said four-thirty. I said, "Uh-uh! This isn't me!" I rolled on over and went back to sleep. And then I overslept.

I get up at five-thirty on school days, because it takes me kind of a long time to do things. So this morning I had to rush to get dressed and eat and have all my books in the book bag by the time the school bus came at eight o'clock.

Daddy had put my wheelchair out front before he went to work, and the bus driver, Mr. Gordon, put it on the bus for me. Then Mrs. Smith, the bus attendant, came to my front door and I held on to her arm and walked to the bus.

I can walk some now, if I hold on to a wall or a piece of furniture or somebody's arm, or if I push my wheelchair. I can even walk a little way without holding on to anything. And I remember when I couldn't do any of those things.

But I don't remember getting hit by that car. I only know what people tell me. My friend Valerie said she had been on the bike with me for a while, but I had let her off just before I started to race with Percy. I'm so glad she got

11

off, so that she wasn't hurt, too. And I'm glad the doctors at the hospital didn't give up on me. They kept working on me and then they came out and said to Daddy and Mama, "We've done all we can. It's up to Alesia and the Lord now, it's up to her and the Lord."

I was unconscious for five weeks. A lot of people were praying for me, and some of them didn't even know me. Mama lit candles in the hospital chapel, and the priests at my church, St. Anthony's, said special prayers. And Sister Clotilde, she had been my teacher that year and I had been so bad in her class, always talking and stuff, but after I got hurt, she had her class praying for me twice a day.

The day I woke up and started to talk, some of the nurses wanted me to surprise Mama. They wanted me to say, "Hi, Mama," when she walked into the room. But Daddy said no, he didn't know if she could stand the shock. So he called her at work and told her the good news. Mama says that after she got off the phone she just said four words—"My child is talking!" And she got out of there and came to the hospital as fast as she could.

I had my tenth birthday party in the hospital on October 8, 1972. I don't remember that, either, but the first time I went back to visit after I got out, something about that hospital smell just struck me. I said, "I remember this smell, yeah, I remember this smell!"

still March 19, 1980

After I went to my morning classes, I ate lunch in the cafeteria. And after that, I went into the activity room and sat and talked to some of my friends. When things got kind of boring, I started telling jokes. Then I went to my afternoon classes, and came home and did my homework in the den, and washed the breakfast dishes. And after dinner, Mama and I went grocery shopping.

My jokes are so corny you just *have* to laugh! When I ask my friends if they want to hear a joke, they say, "No!" Except this one guy in my homeroom class. He tells everybody to be quiet so he can hear the joke, and then after I tell it, he stands up and pretends he's laughing, pretends he's cracking up and stuff. And then I really crack up.

Sat., March 22, 1980

I went to a party at Lisa Hall's house. We really had a good time. The party started at about nine o'clock and wasn't over until three. I danced a lot. But one guy I danced with didn't know I couldn't walk or stand alone, so he let go of me to turn around, and I fell. He helped me up, but I fell down again, so I went and sat on the sofa for a while. Then a nice record came on and Andre and I danced on that one. That was the last record. After that, everybody went home, and I spent the night at Lisa's.

14

Sometimes I have trouble remembering things, but Mama says I never forget about a party I'm going to. I love parties and dancing. On fast music, I stand with my back against the wall and dance. On slow music, I have to put all my weight on the guy. Some guys don't like that. They ask me to dance and then when they find out I have to lean on them, they say, "Never mind." So I say, "Later, much later." I don't waste time with them. I dance with the next one.

One night I went to a high school dance and I saw two of my friends there. They helped me stand against the wall, and I danced with a lot of different guys. Then this one guy asked me to dance, and I said, "Sure." So he said, "You get off that wall!" And he pulled me. My friends got upset, and before I could say anything, they said, "Don't pull her, don't make her fall, she can't walk!" And that was the last thing I wanted him to know. I was going to tell him, "Don't pull me, please, because my back is hurting," or something like that because when most guys find out that I can't walk, they kind of back down. It scares them off before they can get to know me, and I want them to know me first, know what kind of person I am, and then I'll tell them about my disability.

Sun., March 23, 1980

I came back home from Lisa's today, and I went with Daddy and Uncle Roy and my older brother Reid to see the Washington Bullets play basketball against the Detroit Pistons. The last few seconds were *murder!* I was at the edge of my seat just hoping the Bullets would win.

They did, but it sure was a close score.

After I got home, I called Lisa to tell her what a good time I had at her house—the party and everything. Lisa is one of my best friends. We met at Camp Greentop a few years ago. This summer I'm going to have a big cookout, and I've already invited Lisa and Andre and my other Camp Greentop friends. I can't wait for summer to get here.

I was about fifteen the first summer I went to Camp Greentop. I was the only new one, and everybody was so friendly. They said, "Hi, what's your name? How you doing? How'd you get hurt?" They all were disabled, too, so I didn't see any problem with telling them how I got hurt. So I just told them.

I had a whole lot of fun there, putting on shows and going on trips and playing games and stuff. We had a big banquet on the last night and everybody was all sad about going home. Everybody except me. I was still happy. But the next morning, when the buses came to get us, I looked at everybody and just burst out crying. Tears were flying everywhere.

Mon., March 24, 1980

Today seemed to go faster than other Mondays. At school, they called all the eleventh-graders to the library to talk about our schedules for the twelfth grade. We made a list of the subjects we want to take so we can show it to our parents. I might be taking accounting next year. I don't know. But I know I can't wait to be a senior.

Tues., March 25, 1980

Nothing much happened at school today, except work. It's almost time for Easter vacation and I already have homework for over the holidays.

Tomorrow we're supposed to have a party in our Child Study class. That's one of my favorite classes. We're learning all about the unborn baby, and what to do when an infant cries, and how to take care of small children. I like children.

When Mama used to take me grocery shopping in my wheelchair, little children would come up to me and they'd stare and ask a whole lot of questions.

They'd say, "Why are you in that chair?"

I'd say, "Because I can't walk."

"Why can't you walk?"

"Because I got hit by a car."

"Why'd you get hit by a car?"

"Because I rode my bike out in the street."

And then they'd say, "Didn't you know better than to do that?"

I used to get so tickled. But it's not funny when grown folks start staring. You expect it from little children, but not from grown folks. It really gets me when they do it. They could just glance at me and keep on about their business, but they stare so hard, it makes me feel self-conscious.

Some people move way away from me when they see me in the wheelchair, like they're afraid they might catch my disability. They have disabilities, too—faults and things like that, everybody has them. Mine is just more noticeable, but they don't think about it that way.

A lot of people are nice, though. Everywhere I go, whenever I need help, there's always somebody. One time, Mama took me downtown on the subway, and when we got off, the elevator wasn't working, and there was this long, steep flight of steps we had to go up. A man and a woman came over and helped Mama carry me in the chair all the way up those steps. I don't know what we would have done if they hadn't offered to help.

Some people try too hard to help, even when I say I don't need it. Sometimes in a store, I'll be looking at a blouse or something, and somebody will say, "You want me to get that for you?"

I'll say, "No, thank you."

"You want me to push you?"

"No, thank you."

"You want me to . . ."

They just keep asking me even though I say no. I'm glad when people are nice enough to help me when I need it, but I like to do as many things as I can by myself.

Fri., March 28, 1980

I just love Fridays because the next day I get to sleep as late as I want to. And tomorrow, Lisa and I are going to Baltimore for a party. Lisa said they're not going

to wear jeans and stuff, so I'm going to be looking rather nice for this party! I'm so excited!

Today is the last day before Easter vacation. I said goodbye to all my friends at school. I didn't give anybody a kiss the way I did when I was going to Sharpe Health School. I have a lot of good friends here at Woodson, too, but I haven't known them very long. This is my first year at a regular school. I went to Sharpe for six years.

My first day at Sharpe I was scared to death. I was almost in tears. Mama said, "Why are you so scared?" I said, "Because I'm in a wheelchair and everybody will be staring at me." Mama said, "Alesia, *all* the children there are disabled. I don't know why you think they're going to be staring at *you*."

It didn't take me long to get used to everybody. I had missed a year in school, the whole fifth grade, so that's the grade they put me in. I liked Sharpe. I was in a whole lot of plays while I was there. In one play, I was a lawyer. The first time we did that play I won the case, but the second time I lost, and I think I know why. For some reason everything struck me as funny that time. I just kept laughing, I kept smiling, I couldn't help it, and you're supposed to be serious when you're a lawyer. But even my client kept smiling. So the jury voted him guilty.

We had a talent show once, and I sang this song called "We're in Love." I sang along with a Patti Austin record. I don't know why I decided to sing. I could have said a poem, I knew plenty of poems, but I can't sing a little bit. But anyway, Rebecca from the Recreation Department was in charge, and she put me on this high stool on the stage and she said, "Alesia, are you going to be all right?" I said, "Yeah, I'll be cool." So she told me that if I felt like I was going to fall or anything, for me to pull the microphone away from my mouth and she would close the curtains and come and get me.

As soon as the curtains opened and I saw all those people sitting out in the audience, my left leg started jiggling and I started sliding off the stool. I was singing and jiggling and sliding, and I was so nervous I forgot all about

taking the microphone down. Then, after I sang about ten words, I remembered and yanked it down, and somebody closed the curtains real fast and Rebecca ran over and grabbed me. And then she tapped both sides of my face with her hand. I said, "What did you do that for?" She said she thought I was fainting and she was trying to revive me.

The whole thing is really funny to me now, but it sure wasn't funny that day. I was so embarrassed about messing up my act. Rebecca hugged me, and after I calmed down, she put me back out on the stage in a regular chair. When the curtains opened, the audience applauded, and that made me feel a lot better. I got through the song all right that time. I was supposed to move my arms while I sang and put some feeling into it, but I was still too scared to do that. I just sang and got it over with.

Wed., April 2, 1980

We're going to North Carolina sometime this week. Mama and my brother Allen and I are going to visit my grandparents and cousins and everybody. I'm not sure which day we're leaving, but I have my clothes all laid out and ready for the suitcase. When we get there, I hope my cousin Sharon won't be too busy to take me out. I don't know why I'm worrying, she always finds time for me.

My grandparents and I are very good friends. Before Grandma got sick, she used to bake a lot, and I would sample her goodies and scrape the batter bowl. And Grand-daddy and I are about in the same boat—he's not too steady on his feet, either. He was hurt really bad on his job about twelve years ago, and he has to sleep sitting up. He knows what I mean when I say, "I've been sitting so long, my bottom is right numb!"

Sat., April 5, 1980

I'm at Sharon's house. She came to Grandma and Granddaddy's last night and got me. Today we went for a ride and when we got back, we washed Sharon's car. Then her cousin Gerald came over and I helped him wash his car. He has a tape player in the car, and he was *blasting* it!

Tomorrow, I'll be going back home. I still have history homework to do.

Mon., April 7, 1980

Today is Easter Monday. Mama stayed home from work and we went shopping. I need a pair of shoes, the special kind that hook on to the brace I wear on my leg. But the store didn't have my size, so the salesman said he would call us as soon as he gets some in. Then we went to some other stores and I got two pretty sundresses and two pairs of regular shoes. Meanwhile, Allen was getting impatient to get to the jeans store, so that's where we went next.

Shopping for brace shoes isn't any fun. They never have any good styles in those shoes. I don't wear my brace too much now, but I used to have to wear it all the time because my left leg was so weak. The first brace I had was

23

the long kind. It came all the way up to my hip, and that would really mess up my outfits. I had to get big-leg pants, and they weren't even in style then.

When I'm not looking for brace shoes, I love going shopping, especially with my friends. Looking at the different kinds of fashions in the windows. Going in the stores, flipping through the clothes and trying them on, and coming out of the dressing room and saying, "How do I look?"

Wed., April 9, 1980

Today, nothing much to it. I went to school. Nothing there. I want something exciting to happen to me. I can't wait till I learn to really walk again.

Walking, real walking, is gliding. Just gliding along and not thinking about it. Not having to hold on to anything, or wonder whether your knee is going to give out, or worry about stepping on a rock and losing your balance. Walking fast or slow whenever you want to, and when you want to stop, you just put your foot down and stop, and don't have to think, "Should I stop right here or stop right there?" And you don't need any assistance—not a wheelchair or a crutch or anything or anybody. You just glide.

If anybody asked me what I want most in the whole world, I would say, "To be able to walk again." I daydream about it. I can just see myself walking up the street by myself. Without anyone around me. One time I even went

25

so far as to daydream I was running, and I was just so happy.

Sometimes I start thinking about what I would be doing if I could walk. One day I was coming home from visiting my sister, Alexis, and I thought to myself, "Why aren't you walking?" I got choked up, and when we got home I went to my room and fell on my bed and just started crying. I couldn't help it.

Once when I was feeling really down, I asked Mama how she would feel if I just gave up on everything. Mama said, "If you had given up when you were in the hospital, you wouldn't be here now."

Sun., April 13, 1980

I wanted to go to church today, but church starts at eleven-thirty and I didn't wake up until eleven-fifteen. Mama was already dressed and having coffee with Daddy, and I didn't want to make her late. So I just slept for a while longer.

In the evening, Mama and I went outside so I could practice my walking. I have to concentrate on keeping my body straight. And I have to remember to put my foot down the right way. I walk on just the ball of my foot, and you're not supposed to do that. You're supposed to walk on your whole foot, starting with the heel, so I practiced putting my heel down first. I didn't have on my brace, but I guess I did all right because I didn't fall.

One night Mama dreamed I was running across a field like the "Six Million Dollar Man" on television. She

said I started off slow, and then I picked up speed, and the wind got behind me and I was kicking hard, almost flying. And in the dream, Mama was jumping up and down in her nightgown and hollering, "Go, Alesia, go!" When she woke up she was smiling.

27

After the accident, when I was learning how to take steps again, I did the same thing a baby does—I crawled first. Ms. Schiller, the physical therapist at Sharpe, taught me to do it. She said it would make my hands and shoulders and knees stronger. Then, after that, Mama and Alexis taught me to crawl up and down the steps at home so Daddy wouldn't have to carry me anymore. One day I told Mama I wanted to try to walk. I said I thought I could do it, and when Mama asked Ms. Schiller if it would be all right, she said it wouldn't do any harm.

I fell a lot, just like a baby, trying to go from crawling to walking. It was hard on me and hard on Mama, too. She would be holding me, but I was a big girl, I was about twelve, and she couldn't always keep me from falling. One time she was helping me walk from the den to the kitchen—to go to dinner, I think—and all of a sudden my knee gave out. I fell on top of Mama, and my teeth hit the floor. It hurt so bad, I started crying. Mama pretended she wasn't hurt much, but I had on that heavy, long-leg brace, and I know that thing hurt.

I remember the very first time I walked by myself. Alexis was in high school then. She was on the basketball team, and she was going to take me to watch her practice. She went to open the car door for me while I sat in the den, but we were going to be late, so I said to myself, "Let me help her out a little." I decided I would try to walk to the front door.

Nobody else was home, so I had to do it by myself. I was kind of scared, but I wanted to do it, so I pushed up off the arms of my wheelchair and stood up. There wasn't going to be anything for me to hold on to, because if I

leaned over to hold the furniture, I would fall. So I put my mind on walking and nothing else, and I just took a step, and another one, and then about three more, and I was at the door of the den. I grabbed the wall and started smiling, I was so happy I'd made it that far. I looked up to heaven and said, "Thank you."

I stayed there for a minute and got myself together. I was hoping my knee wouldn't give out, so I practiced bending it a little bit, and then I started across the living room. I didn't look in the mirror because I knew it would make me nervous to see myself walking. I looked straight ahead, and I made it to the next wall, and I said, "Thank you" again. Then I had to walk just a few more steps to get to the door—and I did it! I said, "I made it, I made it, thank you!"

I looked out to see where Alexis was. She was coming toward the house, and I was glad she was looking down because when she lifted her head to open the door, I was standing there waving at her. She was so surprised. She burst out laughing and gave me a great big hug. She was still smiling when we got to practice, and everyone was asking me, "What's Alexis smiling so much about?" I said, "I walked to the front door all by myself." They all thought it was nice, but I could tell they didn't really understand why we were so happy.

Daddy is proud of me, but he didn't tell me. He told Alexis and she told me. The day I learned to crawl, he just said, "That's good." But then, later, he told Alexis how proud he felt.

Daddy doesn't get nervous anymore when he sees

me walking. He used to be afraid I would fall and hit my head on something, and he couldn't stand to watch me when I got up out of my chair. He would turn his head away. But now he's getting used to it.

Everybody says Daddy spoils me, but he just likes to make me happy. Some days, when he comes home from work, I show him how I've washed up all the breakfast dishes, and I say, "Daddy, this kitchen is too pretty to mess up." So then he takes us all out to dinner.

Wed., April 16, 1980

I went to a high school basketball game tonight and I met a nice guy. He came over at halftime and said hello and things like that, and after the game was over, he came back to talk some more. We didn't have a chance to talk long because Mama came to get me all early and messed up everything, but he did ask me for those seven little digits—my phone number. I got ready to say no, but before I could get it out, he said, "Let me call you so I can get to know you better." He doesn't know about my disability, so I'll bring it on easy.

Thurs., April 17, 1980

Daddy's sister, Nannie, came over this afternoon and had a nice dinner waiting for us when we got home. After dinner we went over to my brother Reid's. Today is his birthday and we all sang "Happy Birthday" to him.

Everybody at school liked my new navy blue suede sneakers. The second semester is just about half over. It's going by really fast.

31

Sun., April 20, 1980

Reid came over and had breakfast and dinner with us. All day I wanted to go for a ride, but Mama said with gas costing as much as it does, not today. So we went for a walk. Summer is right around the corner because it hit eighty degrees. A lot of people were out enjoying the weather, and I was happy.

Mon., April 21, 1980

Today was a pretty day. It was a little warm, so after I got home from school, I put on my shorts and went outside with some of my friends—and my legs almost froze. I said, "Take me home so I can put on my jeans!" Then we went for a walk around the neighborhood. I'll sure be glad when summer gets here.

I finally made it a point tonight to try to be in bed by eleven-thirty so I won't be so sleepy in the morning.

During the week, my limit on the phone is eleven-thirty, but I usually stay up until about twelve. Everybody else has gone to bed and Mama's fussing, "Why don't you go to bed?"

I say, "I'm not sleepy."

Mama says, "It's going to be hard as the devil to get you up tomorrow morning."

I say, "No, it's not."

How does it end up? Mama's right, it's hard to get me up. Daddy calls me, "Alesia, get up. Alesia, hey Alesia."

I say, "Daddy, please just let me have five more minutes."

32

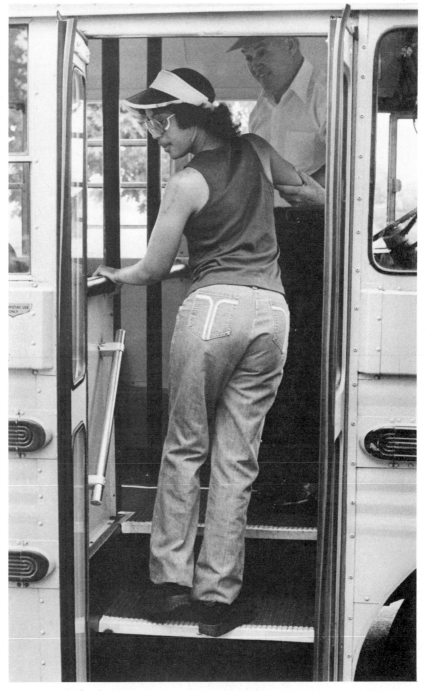

Getting on the bus to go to school isn't easy.

Sometimes I am late getting to class and that makes me feel a little nervous.

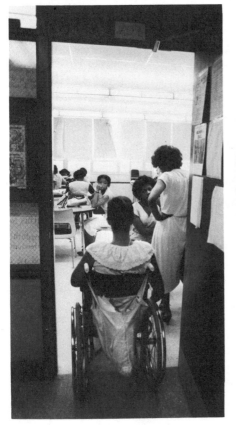

School can be hard work....

....but it has its lighter moments.

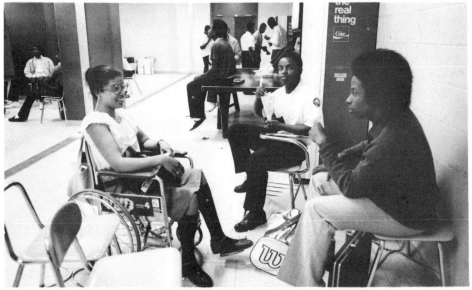

....and it's fun talking with friends in the recreation room.

My mother and I enjoy shopping together.

I like to try on the latest fashions.

Going to church is an important part of our family tradition. Here I am with my mother and father, leaving St. Anthony's Church after Sunday services.

I had a summer job at the Interstate Commerce Commission. Sometimes I did filing.

Making photocopies of reports was fun.

Sometimes we had meetings to discuss things we were working on. I liked it when they asked my opinion.

It takes a lot of work to keep muscles flexible. Here I am at Sharpe School with my physical therapist.

She helps me learn to go down steps by myself.

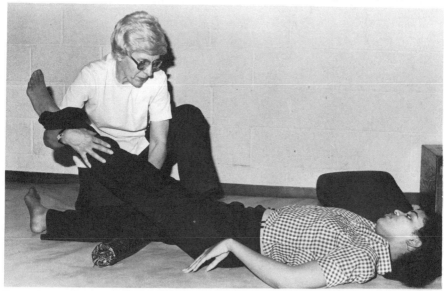

Sometimes therapy hurts, but I have to stretch the muscles in my legs.

I love to dance, and I can do it pretty well if I lean against something for support. This is a dance at St. Luke's.

My friends Dolly and Annette and Valerie, and some of my other friends, used to go for walks with me almost every day in the summer when I was younger. They would push me in the wheelchair, around the block maybe, or sometimes as far as McDonald's. One day Dolly was going to visit her aunt in the hospital and a whole bunch of us went up there with her, and for some reason, as soon as we got in the hospital, Cheryl thought something was funny. She started laughing really hard in the elevator, and then we all started laughing and couldn't stop. I was hoping nobody would get on the elevator with us and thank goodness nobody did.

In North Carolina I used to go for walks uptown with my cousin Sonya. There were all these stores a few blocks from Grandma's house, and most of the time we went to the ten cent store to get candy and stuff. I'd hold on to Sonya's arm and walk up there instead of going in the wheelchair. One time poor Sonya got so tired. I was holding her arm too tight. Sometimes I don't know my own strength.

41

Fri., April 25, 1980

They had an awards ceremony at Howard University Hospital tonight and I was invited. They gave awards to all the young people who worked there last summer. I worked one hundred and forty hours, and when they called my name at the ceremony, I went up to the front to get this pretty certificate.

The job at the hospital was my first job. I sat in front of this big round filing table where I had to put the patients' files. One of the therapists who worked at the hospital came to get some files one day, and she kept turning the table, and turning the table, and I lost my place. I just got everything mixed up and put some files in wrong. I was so mad. But most of the time I did good work.

Some other students from Sharpe worked there too. We had lunch together almost every day, and on my last day Gail gave me a little stuffed rabbit. She said it looked warm and reminded her of me.

Sat., April 26, 1980

Alexis took me to the show tonight to see Chaka Khan and Rufus, Michael Walden and the Brothers Johnson. It was fun! I got up and held on to the rail and danced. Everybody else was all still. I got mad at the people. But I had a good time. I even saw two more people in wheelchairs.

Mon., April 28, 1980

I sure can't say that nothing happened at school today. Something *did* happen. I got stuck on the elevator. Right after I left typing, I got on the elevator to go to my next class, and at first everything was all right. The elevator stopped at the fifth floor to let two teachers off, and Keith and I were going to get off at the seventh, but all of a sudden the elevator stopped between floors. We waited for a minute to see if it would start up again, but it didn't, so we decided to phone for help. Keith made the call, I couldn't reach the phone from my wheelchair. He called the principal's office and told them we were stuck.

They came and banged and clanged on the door, trying to pry it open, and it took almost two hours to get us out! School was out and everything. If I hadn't had some company, I think I would have been scared, but Keith kept on saying funny things. He was saying, "I could be home making me a peanut butter and jelly sandwich," and stuff like that. He kept me laughing the whole time.

My brother Allen can make me laugh without even trying hard. He can just say something, do something, and I start cracking up. I don't know how he does that. Allen's younger than I am, but he helps me a lot. He used to go get snacks for me when I couldn't get them for myself. And he would take me outside in the wheelchair and go find my friends to come and talk to me. And when I was feeling bad because I wanted to do something I couldn't do, he could almost always make me laugh.

43

My mouth used to twist a lot to the left whenever I laughed or smiled. I remember one time when I was in the sixth grade I was talking to some of my friends and somebody said something that made me laugh. Tears came to my eyes, I was laughing so hard, and when I tried to say something, my friends started teasing me, laughing at me,

because I was talking on the side of my mouth. I stopped laughing and I said, "You shouldn't laugh at that, that's not funny." And they said, "We're sorry."

Thurs., May 1, 1980

We're going to North Carolina tomorrow. I'll miss my history quiz, but I know I'll have to take it next week when I get back.

I talked to a friend of mine named Norman tonight. He's graduating from Sharpe and he invited me to go to the prom with him. His sister's going to drive us. I think I'll wear the gown I wore when I was in a popularity contest, the one with the halter top. I hope I can still get in it.

Sat., May 3, 1980

I woke up early because Sharon said she was coming to Grandma's to get me. She said she would pick me up between eight and twelve o'clock, but I couldn't wait. At ten o'clock I called her up and said, "When are you coming!" After she got here we went to get pizza and then we went for a ride with Gerald.

Some people say they're going to take me somewhere, or come over or something, and then they don't do it. One time this friend of mine said he was coming over to my house and I stayed home all that Saturday waiting for him. Mama went out and came back, and so did Alexis and Daddy, and I could have gone with them. But no, I

was stuck in the house. I missed all my Saturday and he never showed up. I could have wrung his neck!

Sometimes I get lonely. Times when there's just nothing to do. Everybody else is busy and I'm the only one that's sitting around. There's nothing on TV, nothing to look at, and I'm just sitting there doing nothing.

Thurs., May 8, 1980

Lisa wants me to go to Virginia with her tomorrow to King's Dominion amusement park. All of my Camp Greentop friends are going, but Mama won't let me leave school early because I already missed a day this week. One more month before school is out. I'm still going to have my big cookout this summer.

Fri., May 9, 1980

Went to a dance with Allen. Had a lot of fun!

Sat., May 10, 1980

Another Saturday is here and gone. I didn't wake up until twelve-something. I missed "American Bandstand," but I did get to see "Soul Train." Jermaine Jackson was on. He finally let his hair back to a natural.

I made the menu today for my cookout. And I've got just about everything planned. I want to have it in Rock Creek Park near the water. We can go for a walk

47

and play checkers and cards and stuff. All I have to do now is pick a day.

Sun., May 11, 1980

Today was Mother's Day. Daddy woke me up to go to church, but I didn't get up right away. Mama got dressed, and Allen fixed breakfast, and *then* I decided to get up. We ended up leaving the house about two minutes before church was supposed to start. Mama was so mad at me, you could have fried an egg on top of her head.

After church, we went to our friends', the Malloys, for Mother's Day dinner. They had big Jumbo crab legs over rice, salad, corn, broccoli, punch and little cakes. I ate until I got full, and then when I got home I wanted to eat again, but I didn't do it because I have this new dress to wear to my cousin Yvette's wedding and I don't want to eat myself out of it.

Mon., May 12, 1980

We get to wear shorts to school tomorrow. Mr. Breckenridge, our assistant principal, reminded us over the loudspeaker this afternoon that tomorrow is Olympics Day.

I read in the paper that this scary picture, "Silent Scream," is at the movies. I want to see it, but somebody's got to stay there with me because I'm not sitting through that by myself!

I went to a haunted house once with Alexis. It was

48

on the boardwalk in Ocean City, Maryland. We walked through it and looked around at all the things that were supposed to be scary, and I wasn't even scared. I laughed at everything. Then Alexis helped me up these three steps, and there was this coffin. It had a dead man in it, he was made of wax or something, and he was the color of chalk. And there were cobwebs and spiderwebs and everything. I said, "Take me down! Take me down!" Alexis said, "I thought you wanted to see it." I said, "I've seen enough! Take me down!"

Tues., May 13, 1980

I only went to my first three classes because after lunch we had the Olympics in our stadium. They had different kinds of races, and even the teachers ran in some of them. I parked my wheelchair in front of the gate so I could pull myself up and stand up and watch.

At Sharpe the boys had a wheelchair basketball team called the Dolphins. Every time they played I would have Mama sit me over with the cheerleaders, and I would do the cheers with them. Some of us were in wheelchairs and some were on crutches and we'd yell, "We love, we love those Dolphins, we love, we love those Dolphins, deep down in our hearts, talkin' about deep deep, oh, down down, deep down in our hearts, talkin' about deep down in our hearts!"

I remember one time the game was almost over and we were a little bit behind. It was the last few seconds. Eric got the ball and rolled down the court and nobody

49

could catch him. He shot that ball and it didn't even spin around in the hoop, it went straight through the net, and we won. *Everybody* was screaming, even Mama.

Sat., May 17, 1980

We went to Richmond for my cousin Yvette's wedding. Her gown was really pretty. And the flower girl and the ring bearer were so cute. Some weddings last forever and ever, but this one was nice and short. After the reception, all the guests went outside and waited for Yvette and Alvin to come out. We had rice all ready for them. I stood at the end, beside the car, so I'd be the last one to throw my rice, and after everybody else had thrown theirs, and Alvin had opened the car door for Yvette to get in, I said, "Hey, Yvette!" She looked at me and I threw my rice right at her. Everybody laughed.

Fri., May 23, 1980

Norman had on a navy blue suit when he came to get me. He looked *good*. And me myself was looking rather nice too, in my halter gown! We were stepping out, going to the prom. Alexis took a picture of me coming downstairs, and then she took pictures of Norman and me together before we left.

The prom was held in Sharpe's gym. I saw a lot of my old friends, and we were just hugging. Everybody had a good time at the prom. One time the d.j. looked over at me and I said, "Play Michael Jackson's 'Off the Wall.' " He played it, and he even played another cut by Michael, and that was fine with me! After the prom was over, we

50

all went in the teachers' cars to the Pancake House and ate, and then I called Daddy to come and get us, and he took Norman home, and we came home, and that was the end of a perfect day.

Thurs., May 29, 1980

I went up to Sharpe today to see Ms. Schiller, my physical therapist. I had to get my heel cord stretched. That's that cord at the back of your foot that connects your heel to your leg. Mine was tight because I hadn't been to therapy for a while. It was so tight I couldn't put my heel down on the floor. Ms. Schiller pulled it and it hurt so much I felt like crying. But I knew she was trying to help me, so I just stayed pretty much cool. And after she had finished, my heel could touch the floor.

I do exercises every night just before I go to bed. I exercise my arms, and I pull my knee up to my chest ten times, and I cross my right foot over my left and my left foot over my right. And I do twists, fifty on each side, because I wouldn't mind having a slim waist.

When I was a student at Sharpe, I had to go to the physical therapy room almost every day so Ms. Schiller could help me do all the things I needed to do to improve— sit-ups, rolling on a mat from one end to the other, things like that. I used to love the scooter board. That's a board with four small wheels on it, two in front and two in back. I would lie on my stomach on two scooter boards, because I was kind of tall, and I'd push myself up this ramp, get to the top, turn around, and come flying back down.

Thurs., June 26, 1980

Summer is definitely here because I started on my summer job today, at the Interstate Commerce Commission. I work in the personnel office. Everybody there is nice. One man is deaf, and he's going to teach me some sign language. I know I won't get bored at work because I have a lot to do. I go on errands, make copies on the copy machine, file charts, and sometimes I answer the phone. When I pick up the phone, I say "Personnel" in a sweet voice.

Sat., June 28, 1980

Daddy, Mama and I went to the beach at Ocean City, Maryland, today. I had a nice time, lying on the sand and getting in the water. We had a late dinner, a crab cake sandwich for me. Then I watched television and went to bed.

Once when I was about twelve and we were in Ocean City with some friends, I wore shorts to the beach. I didn't wear my bathing suit because I thought we were going to the boardwalk, but instead, everybody went down to the beach. So I said, "I want to go back and get my bathing suit." Mama said, "It's too far. Go ahead and get in the water in your shorts." So she walked me to the edge of the beach, and I sat down right there in the water and let the waves come up and smack me in the face.

Sun., June 29, 1980

It was scary on the road coming back to D.C. The sky was ocean-color blue, and there was a whole lot of lightning and thunder before the rain came. But we made it home all right.

I finally picked a day for my cookout. I'm going to have it this coming Saturday in my back yard. I was going to ask Lisa Hall to bring some of her records, but she can't come. She'll be away at Camp Greentop.

I don't know why, but for some reason, this evening, I keep thinking about this guy I know. He's way out in another state, and I just keep thinking about him.

Tues., July 1, 1980

I walked a lot at work yesterday, by pushing my wheelchair instead of riding in it, and now my leg hurts. I remember what Ms. Schiller told me, that if I do too much walking, my leg will get sore. And sure enough, that's what happened. So today, I rode all day.

A couple of weeks ago, I was pushing my wheelchair down the hall, going to run off some copies, and I guess my foot hit one of the rails in back of the chair, and the chair tipped backward and went down, and I went down, too. My co-workers helped me up. I didn't get hurt, I'm glad of that.

Sat., July 5, 1980

A whole lot of things went wrong at my cookout. I had been looking forward to it ever since I first thought of having it, and it didn't turn out right. First of all I picked a bad time to have it, a holiday weekend. Just about everybody was going to be out of town or somewhere with their families. But a few people said they thought they could come, so Mama and I fixed the food. I strung the beans and helped make the potato salad.

Andre had called from Baltimore to say that his bus was leaving at two fifty-five, but I got it mixed up and told Mama that that was when he would *arrive.* Mama drove me to the bus station, and we waited and waited, and no Andre. So we went back home, and Allen put his hi-fi on the back porch, and he and Daddy took the food outside. The table looked really nice. Then, all of a sudden, out of a clear blue sky, a big rainstorm came up, great big sheets of rain.

The rain didn't last but a couple of minutes, but that was long enough to mess things up. Daddy and Allen ran out in the rain to get everything, but it was too late for the tablecloth and some of the food. The bacon strips

were floating in the baked beans. It was a mess. Then Andre called and said he was at the station, so Mama and I went to pick him up.

Andre was the only one who could make it, and I was glad he came. We ate the food that didn't get wet, and played cards and talked and watched TV. So we had fun anyway, even if it wasn't a real cookout.

Wed., August 13, 1980

A friend of mine named Sylvester came down to my office to have lunch with me today. When we left the cafeteria, we had to go through this corridor where the floor slopes uphill. It wasn't easy in our wheelchairs. My arms gave out, and then Sylvester said, "Hold on to my chair," and he pulled both of us. I should have held on with my left hand because my right arm is stronger and I could have helped roll my chair, but by the time I thought of it, we were halfway up the hill, and I was afraid that if I tried to switch hands I would roll backward and get hurt. Anyway, we made it. We got through it with nobody else's help and I was so proud of us.

Tues., September 2, 1980

It's the first day of school. I'm a senior!

I can't decide what I want to do after graduation. I might go to college, but I've been going to these places that help you decide on a career and they all say that I would do well in a personnel office. A few years ago I wanted to be a lawyer, then a nursery school teacher. Then I wanted to be a model, but I said to myself, "Nobody ever heard of a disabled model." So I dropped that from my list. But now I'm kind of thinking of it again. Mama says I have pretty hands and maybe I could model my hands. I guess I'll have to make up my mind pretty soon.

Wed., October 8, 1980

Today is my birthday, my eighteenth birthday. At lunchtime I was in the activity room, sitting at a table with Thomas, and when I told him it was my birthday, he went out into the middle of the room and said, "Hey y'all, today is Alesia's birthday!" Then he came back to the table and said, "How did you like that?" And in homeroom class, Danny came over and kissed me on the cheek and said, "Happy Birthday!"

This evening, Daddy, Mama, Allen and Alexis took me out to dinner to celebrate. Then Alexis baked me a cake, a vanilla cake with white icing, and everybody sang "Happy Birthday" to me.

I'm a woman now, I'm not a girl anymore. I keep thinking about that. In three years I'll be twenty-one. In less than one year I'll be out of high school. I've just about decided to go to college. If I do, I want to live on campus. I want to get used to being out in the world and see what I can do on my own.

When I was in the accident, after I woke up from the coma and got a little better, I left Providence Hospital and went to the Hospital for Sick Children. I could use my

58

right hand, I could feed myself, but that was about all I could do on my own. My whole body was so limp that my neck wouldn't even hold my head up. There was this green, collarlike thing on the back of the wheelchair to keep my head from just falling from one side to the other, and Daddy and Mama would turn my head for me so I could look at them when they came to see me.

My family says I'm not always as independent as I could be. Like, Mama says I could roll my hair up if I tried. I roll up the front, but I don't do the back, because my left arm gets tired. Mama says if I practiced enough I could do it. I tell her, "My hair doesn't look right when I do it." But she still says, "Practice makes perfect."

It helps you to do things when you have people pulling for you. You're pulling for yourself, of course, but then you have other people pulling for you, too. Your family and friends and everybody. You know if you don't try, you let them down. They've gone out of their way trying to please you and everything, and then you just sit there and don't try, it kind of puts them down.

Sometimes I worry about what my future is going to be like. But then, I know that it's going to be all right. When I was in the hospital, unconscious, the doctors told Mama and Daddy that if I lived, I would probably be like a vegetable for the rest of my life. I wouldn't be able to think or care about things or laugh or anything. But it didn't happen that way. I'm not a vegetable, I'm a person. And I'm still here, still living.

Fri., October 24, 1980

Things are getting exciting. Next month we're having a Senior Class Tea for our parents. Daddy and Mama are coming, and I'm *sure* not going to miss it.

We had our homecoming dance at school tonight. I hung out with my friends, Mary and Katherine. When we went out on the dance floor, I looked at them to see what dance they were doing, and I held on to Mary's shoulder and did the same thing. And I didn't fall once. Some of my other friends were there too, watching, and everybody was proud of me. I can't wait until they see me on graduation day. I've been practicing, and I'm almost sure that I am going to walk all the way across that stage by myself to get my diploma. Maybe with my cane. But not holding on to anybody's arm. Nobody around me, waiting to catch me. Just me myself, Alesia.

Eloise Greenfield has received many honors for her distinguished books for young readers. She has been called "a national treasure" by the Interracial Books for Children Bulletin, which has presented her with a special citation for her "outstanding and exemplary contribution in...children's literature." Mrs. Greenfield lives in Washington, D.C., not far from Alesia Revis.

George Ford has illustrated many outstanding books including Eloise Greenfield's *Paul Robeson*. In 1974, he was, with Sharon Bell Mathis, a winner of the Coretta Scott King Award. Mr. Ford lives in Brooklyn, New York, with his wife, a children's book editor, and their young daughter.

Sandra Turner Bond is an editor and photographer based in Washington, D.C. Her photographs have appeared in newspapers and association publications in Washington and Boston. She has exhibited widely and is a founding member of *Selective Focus*, a Black women's photography collective.